THE WORLD TURNS RED

TIM WAGGONER

Cemetery Dance Publications

Baltimore

❧ 2025 ❧

THE WORLD TURNS RED

Cemetery Dance Publications
132B Industry Lane, Unit #7
Forest Hill, MD 21050
www.cemeterydance.com

Trade Paperback Edition
ISBN: 978-1-964780-34-4

Praise for Tim Waggoner

"I like reading Tim Waggoner books. I'm never *quite* sure what I'm going to get, other than something that's bound to be a wild ride, unexpected turns, completely gruesome moments, and humor both bright and dark."

— Looking For a Good Book

"Waggoner, more than any horror writer that I've read, regularly takes the reader to a dark Wonderland, and I absolutely love the trip."

— Looking For a Good Book

"His ability to weave the surreal with the hyperreal is his greatest talent."

— Signal Horizon

"Tim Waggoner excels in building up a surreal sense of dread, blurring the boundaries between otherworldly horror and everyday tragedy with unnerving finesse."

— CITY NOMADS

"Bram Stoker Award winner Tim Waggoner consistently delivers the goods when it comes to hard-hitting horror fiction, with compelling characters and dangerous horrors at every turn."

— THIS IS HORROR

"Tim Waggoner manages to meld surreal imagery and events with strong character work and an immersive point of view, resulting in work that shocks you on the surface and unsettles you right down to your bones."

— FEARnet

This one's for everyone who's ever heard the voice of the Unhigh. You are not alone.

THE WORLD TURNS RED

Lewis Cooper is sitting at his dining table, laptop open in front of him, grading essays for his Intro to Sociology class, when he detects movement from the corner of his eye. He turns to look out the window and sees Clay Burns, his across-the-street neighbor, toss a rope over the lowest limb of the old oak tree standing in his yard. Clay is in his late sixties, and his young grandson – Lewis can't remember the kid's name – stands next to Clay, watching. The boy is so excited he's practically jumping up and down, and he has a big grin on his face. So does Clay.

That's when Lewis realizes the rope ends in a noose.

Not a full-fledged hangman's noose, but a simple loop with a slipknot. Lewis notices two additional details then: the other end of the rope is tied around the base of the tree, and a stepladder stands on the ground directly beneath the noose. A cold sensation punches him in the gut and rapidly spreads through his body. He sits frozen, hands poised above his keyboard, watching as Clay walks over to examine the noose. He tugs on it to make sure it's secured firmly to the tree, checks the slipknot to see if it's tight and moves easily. Evidently satisfied, he turns to his grandson and spreads his arms, as if saying *See this wonderful thing that I've made?*

Lewis' mind races. It's the first Saturday in October, so Clay's probably decorating for Halloween. Never mind that in the nine years Lewis has lived in his home, he's never known Clay to decorate his yard for any holiday. There's a first time for everything, right? The noose is the only decoration, though – no plastic skeletons or inflatable ghosts, not even a goddamned pumpkin. Perhaps those things will come later.

Perhaps they won't.

For a moment, Lewis is a young boy himself, standing in the living room of his childhood home, looking at his father sitting in his favorite chair, head a bloody ruin, gun still gripped in his dead hand, arm dangling over the chair's arm.

Lewis is up and running for the front door before he's aware of moving. He races out of the dining room, through the living room, reaches the front door, grips the knob, turns, pulls, but the door refuses to open. He yanks it hard, once, twice, before realizing the damn thing is locked. He undoes the chain, turns the deadbolt, and this time when he tries to open the door, it obeys. He steps onto his porch, bare feet cold on concrete, and shouts, "Don't do it!" He's not sure who he's yelling to – Clay, the boy, or both.

In the time it took him to run from the dining room to the porch, Clay's grandson has climbed the stepladder. He stands on the top step now, and Clay places the noose over the boy's head, the action deliberate, almost reverent. He tightens the noose, then steps back, head tilted to the side, as if examining his work for flaws. He nods, satisfied. Neither Clay nor the boy reacted to Lewis' initial shout, so he tries again, louder this time.

"Stop! It's not safe!"

Clay and the boy turn to look at him this time. They're still grinning, so wide now that it seems their lips might split and the corners of their mouths tear. Then the boy waves at Lewis and jumps.

Lewis lets out a cry that's half moan, half scream.

The stepladder falls backward, and the rope pulls taut as the boy falls. The branch the rope hangs over isn't more than eight feet off the ground, but it's thick and sturdy, and high enough that the boy's feet only graze the grass beneath him. Lewis expects the boy to thrash wildly, legs kicking, hands clawing at the rope around his throat in a desperate attempt to loosen it, but he does none of these things. Instead, he hangs relaxed as his body sways back and forth, still grinning, gaze fixed firmly on Lewis.

Do something!

Lewis wants to, desperately, but he's in the grip of a full-bore panic attack now, and can't move. His heart thunders in his chest, and his lungs refuse to work. There's a roaring in his ears, and he feels dizzy and light-headed. Is he going to pass out? Part of him hopes so, because then he won't have to look at the dying boy any longer, but that mercy is denied him. He remains conscious, unable to look away as the boy's face reddens, turns purple, grin relaxing into a thin, straight line. Life lingers in the boy's eyes longer than it should, but eventually the light dims, and the eyes become dull and glassy.

Lewis' paralysis breaks then, and he steps off the porch and begins walking across his lawn, stride measured, movements mechanical. Is he in shock? He thinks it likely. Meanwhile, Clay's clapping, as if his grandson just gave the performance of his life. *Or his death,* Lewis thinks, and he feels a hysterical giggle bubbling up from deep inside. It takes everything he has to keep it from bursting out.

When he reaches Clay's lawn, the older man gives him a friendly wave without taking his eyes off his grandson's corpse swaying in the breeze.

"Hey, Lewis! Lovely day, isn't it? Feels almost like summer."

It *is* warm out, somewhere in the low seventies, but Lewis feels cold, damn cold, like he's a thin layer of skin stretched over a block of ice.

"What did . . . Why . . . We have to . . ."

Lewis' brain is a malfunctioning circuit, sputtering, sparking, unable to complete a coherent thought. He doesn't know Clay well, just enough to wave hi whenever they're both working in their yards. On rare occasions they exchange banalities about the neighborhood – teenagers who drive too fast on the street, people who allow their cats to run loose, dog owners who let their pets shit in other people's yards without picking it up, weekend partiers who make too much noise after nine p.m. . . . . Other than Clay's opinions about these less-than-world-shattering issues, Lewis knows almost nothing about the man. He has a wife – Patti – and at least one child, a daughter who is mother to the dead boy hanging from the oak tree in Clay's front yard. Clay's retired, but Lewis isn't certain what profession the man was in.

Heating and air-conditioning repair maybe, or something like that. But nothing in their exchanges, as few and brief as they were, so much as hinted that Clay was capable of killing his own grandson. *Helping* kill, he amends. The boy mounted the stepladder willingly enough – or so it seemed – and he jumped without any urging or provocation from Clay. The boy, with his grandfather's assistance, committed suicide. It's an insane thought, but Lewis can find no other explanation for the horrific event he witnessed . . . and failed to prevent.

Daddy? Are you okay? Daddy?

Maybe Clay's mad, the boy too. The way they grinned like lunatics as they'd worked together to end the boy's life . . . Clay's still smiling even now, though not as broadly as before.

A breeze kicks up then, dislodging a dozen or so brown leaves from the oak, sending them drifting down around the hanging boy. The wind brings with it the stink of feces and urine, and Lewis knows the boy shit and pissed himself as he'd died.

With an effort, Lewis forces his thoughts to coalesce.

"We have to call the police."

His voice is a monotone and the cadence of his words is off, but at least he manages to get them out.

"Why?" Clay says. For the first time since Lewis' arrival, Clay looks at him. "Is something wrong? Are you alright?"

Lewis feels something snap inside him.

"Fuck no, I'm not alright! I just watched you hang your goddamn grandson! Are you *insane?* Do you have any idea what you've *done?*"

Lewis looks at him a moment, expression unreadable, and then he laughs.

"I did exactly what I was supposed to."

Lewis experiences a nearly overwhelming urge to fasten his hands around Clay's throat and squeeze, but then a wet, thick voice says, *"That's right. He did."*

Even distorted as it is, Lewis recognizes the voice. He doesn't want to look, would give anything not to, but his body turns toward the speaker anyway, as if compelled by an outside force. His father – dead for nearly four decades – stands there, wearing the same flannel shirt and jeans he had on *that day*, the clothes splattered with crimson. His head, what remains of it after the shotgun shell did its work, is a lopsided mess of blood, bone, and meat. The mouth is mostly intact, blood bubbling from it as he breathes. A thought cuts through Lewis' horrified revulsion: since when do ghosts need to take in oxygen? His father holds the shotgun he used to end his life in one hand, muzzle pointed toward the ground, the weapon's metal gleaming in the sunlight.

Lewis hears a car coming down the street, engine loud and rough, as if the driver has mashed the accelerator to the floor. Another of the damn teenagers that use their neighborhood as a race track, Lewis guesses. He turns toward the sound, grateful to be distracted from Clay, the hanged boy, and the too-real apparition of his dead father. A red pickup races toward them, the vehicle not one that Lewis recognizes as belonging to any of his neighbors. He wishes the driver were going slower, not for safety's sake, but because the longer it takes for the pickup to pass Clay's house, the longer Lewis can avoid thinking about Clay's grandson and his father.

As the pickup draws closer, Clay shouts, "My turn!" and runs into the street, moving with surprising speed for a man his age. He turns toward the approaching vehicle, spreads his arms wide, and grins as death bears down upon him. Lewis shouts Clay's name and runs toward the man, intending to grab hold of his arm and yank him out of the pickup's path, or perform a flying tackle and knock the crazy bastard out of danger's way. But he barely manages to reach the sidewalk when the pickup slams into Clay at full speed. There's a dull *whump*, and Clay flies into the air, body limp, a cloth doll stuffed with rags. The driver slams on the brakes then, and the pickup screeches to a stop as Clay hits the asphalt, bounces, rolls, and then lays still. The man's arms and legs are bent at unnatural angles, blood flows from his mouth and ears, and his skull is caved in on one side.

The driver's side door of the pickup opens, and a woman gets out – late thirties, wearing a gray jacket, skirt, and black flats, as if she were on her way to work, a pistol gripped tight in her right hand. She walks toward Clay, gun held down at her side, and stops when she reaches him. Incredibly, given the severity of his injuries, Clay still lives. He gazes up at the woman, the fingers on his right hand twitching, as if he wants to reach toward her but is unable to lift his arm to do so. The woman raises the gun and aims it at Clay's now-misshapen head.

"Want me to finish the job?" she asks. "Or would you rather linger a while and enjoy the pain?"

Sound comes out of Clay's mouth as a liquid cough, blood stippling the asphalt near his face.

"Ling . . . errrr . . ."

"Suit yourself."

The woman presses the gun muzzle to her temple and pulls the trigger.

"THIS ISN'T HAPPENING."

"Sorry, kiddo, but it really is."

Lewis spins around, sees his father grinning at him with blood-slick teeth.

"You're not real! Leave!"

His father laughs, the sound coming out as a wet, gurgling wheeze.

"If I'm not real, how can I go anywhere?"

"Just do it!"

The apparition vanishes. The kid dangling at the end of the rope is still there, though, and still just as dead as before. Lewis turns back toward the street, his entire body trembling. *Breathe, just breathe . . .* He closes his eyes and concentrates on taking several slow, deep breaths, and while he doesn't stop shaking entirely when he's done, he feels a bit more in control of himself. He opens his eyes, looks up and down the street, sees no one else standing on their porch, in their yard, or on the sidewalk. Surely *someone* in the neighborhood heard all the noise – the pickup's racing engine, the impact when the vehicle struck Clay, the squealing tires as the woman swerved to a stop, the gunshot when she killed herself. But no one has left their houses to investigate. *Maybe they're too afraid*, he thought. *Or maybe they've all gone crazy, too.*

He doesn't want to consider that last possibility.

The twisted, broken thing that Clay has become moans as it struggles to raise its head. Lewis doesn't want to go near the dying man. What if what happened was caused by some kind of illness? If Lewis comes too close to Clay, he might catch it, and then he'd be the one trying to kill himself. No way in hell is he going to take that risk, not with Clay bleeding like that, potentially filling the air with whatever virus he contracted.

"Lew . . . issssss . . ." Clay breathes.

"Fuck you," Lewis says softly, then turns his back on his neighbor.

Despite the day's warmth, he feels chilled, and he crosses his arms over his chest to hold in some measure of his body heat. It doesn't help. Whatever has happened here, it's too much for him to deal with. He needs to call the police. Hopefully, someone else in the neighborhood is aware that something bad has happened and has already called 911, and while he's tempted to leave it at that, head back to his house, go inside, lock the front door, and hide from the world – forever, if need be – he knows he can't do that. He and Clay weren't friends, not to mention the sonofabitch helped kill his own grandson, but Lewis *did* witness the man's death, as well as the kid's and the pickup driver's, and he has a responsibility to report what he's seen to the authorities. And once he does, this fucking mess will become *their* problem, and Lewis can get busy day drinking and pretend none of this happened.

As if he could ever forget.

His phone is in his house, lying on the dining table next to his laptop. He doesn't know if Clay has a land-line, but given the man's age, he thinks it likely, and his house is closer. He can ask Clay's wife . . .

Christ. Clay's *wife*.

Patti.

He turns to face the front door to Clay's house. It's closed, but he doubts it's locked. Maybe Patti isn't home. He knows her even less well than he did Clay, but she always seems to be going somewhere. Whenever he sees their SUV backing out of the garage, invariably Patti is behind the wheel. What if Clay did something to Patti before ushering his grandson outside and helping the boy hang himself? What if she's hurt and needs help? Lewis knows he isn't thinking straight, that he can't be after the deaths he witnessed, but it seems to him that if there's any chance at all that he can save Patti's life, he has to try.

He walks to the front door, grips the knob, hesitates only a moment, and then goes inside. Clay has never invited Lewis into his home, and as he stands in the vestibule, he feels like he's intruding into a space where he doesn't belong. The smell of fried bacon lingers in the air, and Lewis guesses Clay or Patti made breakfast earlier. The aroma causes his stomach to gurgle – it's nearly lunchtime – and he feels as if his body has betrayed him. How can he possibly be hungry after what he's seen? But the body wants what it wants when it wants it, and to hell with everything else. Survival is the name of the game, and the body's determined to continue functioning at all costs. At least his is, and he takes comfort in that. Whatever caused Clay, his grandson, and the SUV driver to take their own lives hasn't gotten to him. Not yet, anyway.

"Mrs. Burns?" he calls out, then "Patti?"

No response. The silence is heavy, oppressive, and he experiences a sudden urge to turn around and get the hell out of there. Instead, he moves further into the house. It's a typical ranch home, same as his, and has a similar layout: the vestibule leads to a living room on the left, then to a hallway, with the kitchen off to the right. Patti isn't in the living room, so he continues on to the kitchen, and that's where he finds her. She lies on the tiled floor in front of the sink, facedown, left arm beneath her, right arm stretched out, as if she's reaching for something. Blood covers the floor, as well as the sink counter, and when Lewis sees the mangled ruin that was Patti's right hand, his stomach lurches, and hot bile sears the back of his throat. He understands what happened. Patti jammed her hand into the garbage disposal and then bled to death from the resulting injury. She *looks* dead, anyway. Lewis knows he should step over to her, kneel down, touch his fingers to her throat, and check her pulse, but to do so would mean stepping in her blood, and he can't make himself do that.

He becomes aware of a low hum then and realizes it's coming from the sink. The disposal is still on, but something has caused it to jam, most likely one of Patti's fingers.

Gray nibbles at the edges of his vision then, and he sways, suddenly dizzy. He's never blacked out before, but he thinks he's on the verge of doing so now. The only thing that allows him to hold onto consciousness is the thought that if he falls, he'll likely land in Patti's blood. He sweeps his gaze around the area, searching for a phone, finding none.

Fuck this. Go back to your place and use your phone.

Excellent advice, he decides. He turns and heads back toward the front door, the metallic smell of blood thick in his nostrils.

"335 Holcombe Lane. Yes, I'll be here. Thank you."

Lewis ends the call and puts his phone down on the dining table, relieved the situation is now a police matter. He'll have to give a statement to the officers when they arrive, but once he does that, he'll no longer be involved. He's so grateful, he could weep. He'll need to avoid the reporters who'll turn up when they learn about the multiple suicides. No way in hell does he want to be part of the media feeding frenzy that will descend on his neighborhood. After he speaks with the police, all he'll want is to be left alone so he can begin processing the horrors he saw.

He's sitting in front of his laptop again, and he moves the tip of his index finger across the mouse pad to bring the screen back to life. He's still logged in to his Intro to Sociology course page, but there's no way he'll be able to concentrate and continue grading essays. He logs out of the site and does a search for psychologists in the area. He's going to need a good therapist to help him deal with the trauma he's experienced, and if he can't find someone this way, maybe he'll ask Flora for a recommendation. He begins perusing websites and patient reviews, but while his eyes take in text and photos, none of the information makes any real impression on him. In his mind, he keeps seeing the boy hanging from the rope, face turning purple, Clay running into the street to be struck by the SUV, the vehicle's driver getting out and shooting herself in the head, Patti lying on her kitchen floor, right hand nothing but mangled meat and crushed bone. But most of all, he sees his father standing in the Burns' yard, a grisly specter with only half a head, clothes splashed with crimson.

And he remembers.

"CAN WE GO TO THE PARK TODAY?" LEWIS ASKS. He's seven years old.

"Maybe later."

Robert Cooper sits on a gray upholstered couch that sags in the middle, facing a small TV, watching a baseball game with the sound muted. He holds the remote in his right hand, as if he intends to change the channel any moment, but Lewis knows he won't. Once his daddy starts watching a game, he sticks with it until it's over. *I'm a finisher,* he once told Lewis, and while Lewis wasn't sure what he meant, he nodded, feigning understanding. Daddy hasn't lived in this apartment long – only a couple of weeks – and the place still smells of fresh paint. *They always paint an apartment and clean the carpets before someone moves in,* Daddy told him the first time Lewis came to visit. *It's supposed to give the illusion that the place is new, that no one else has ever lived here before – which is bullshit, of course.*

Lewis doesn't like the apartment. It's much smaller than their house – Mommy's house now – and it doesn't have a yard for him to play in. All it has is a parking lot, and Daddy doesn't want him playing there. *You never know when some dumbass will be driving through the complex too fast and not paying attention to what the fuck they're doing. Plus, a lot of people live here too, and not all of them are nice, if you know what I mean.*

Lewis didn't, but he does as Daddy asked and stays inside whenever he's here – Wednesday nights and every other weekend. The problem is, there isn't much to do here. The living room is so small it barely counts as a room at all, as far as Lewis is concerned. There's only one bedroom, and Daddy lets him sleep on the bed and takes the couch whenever Lewis stays over. The bed's lumpy and smells funny. Daddy said he got it at a hotel overstock store, whatever that is. That's where all his furniture came from – couch, coffee table, small dining table with two rickety chairs, a floor lamp for the living room, a desk lamp for the nightstand in the bedroom. *Not exactly the Ritz, huh?* Daddy said when he first showed Lewis around the apartment. Lewis had no idea what the Ritz was, but he said, *No, it isn't.*

Daddy looked hurt when he said this, although Lewis wasn't sure why.

Lewis wants to ask Daddy how much later *later* will be. It's a sunny spring day, and he really-really-*really* wants to go to the park. But he knows Daddy doesn't like it when he pesters him, so he says nothing. He sits cross-legged on the floor and pretends to watch the game, although he doesn't find sports interesting in the slightest. *Playing* games he can understand. That's fun. But *watching* other people play games? What's the point of that? He wishes Daddy would buy a video game system so they can play games together, but he said it's too expensive and that Lewis already has a system at his mother's place with a dozen different games. Lewis would bring the system and games with him whenever he comes, but for some reason, Mommy won't let him. He doesn't understand why, but he's only seven, and he's used to not understanding things, especially grown-ups.

Daddy bought one new thing, though, and it sits propped up against the left side of the couch. A shotgun. A real one, not a toy. Lewis isn't sure when Daddy got it – it just showed up one day – and he isn't allowed to touch it, which sucks. But when Daddy makes a rule, he expects Lewis to follow it, and Lewis – who wants to be a good boy – always does what Daddy says. Most of the time, anyway. When he asked Daddy why he got a shotgun, he said, *Protection*, and refused to answer any more questions about it. He always keeps the shotgun near him in the apartment, even when he sleeps, and he takes it in the car with him whenever he drives anywhere. Lewis figures Daddy must need a *lot* of protecting.

Sometimes Daddy holds the shotgun in his lap and strokes the metal barrel as if the weapon is a beloved pet. Once Lewis came out of the bathroom to find Daddy standing in the middle of the living room, holding the shotgun with the muzzle in his mouth. When Daddy realized he was there, he pulled the shotgun away from his face and smiled. *I just wanted to see how it tastes*, he said. Lewis got a fluttery feeling in his stomach when Daddy said this, but he told himself that adults are weird and tried to put the incident out of his mind.

After several moments of watching the game, Lewis says, "Who do we want to win?"

"I don't care," Daddy says.

"Then why are you watching?"

"I'm waiting."

"For what?"

"To see what happens. I've got a decision to make, and the outcome of this game is going to help me."

Daddy's tone is flat and emotionless as he says this. Lewis thinks he sounds like a robot, and for the next several minutes, he imagines what it would be like to be a human kid with a robot father. It would be pretty cool, especially if Daddy had awesome robot powers like super strength and super speed – and if he were a robot, he could probably jump really high, and he'd have a computer brain, too.

Lewis doesn't understand why his parents got divorced. He isn't even sure what the word means, other than that they don't live together anymore and don't like to talk to each other. They tried to explain, told him that it wasn't anybody's fault, that they *grew apart* and *wanted different things out of life,* but no matter what, they'd always love him and still be his Mommy and Daddy. They also told him that sometimes when parents divorce, the kids think it happened because they'd done something wrong. But they assured him he didn't do anything to cause their divorce, and while he has his doubts, he does his best to believe his parents.

Mommy adjusted to their new situation more easily than Daddy. She smiles a lot more, and sometimes she sings when doing chores around the house. She has a new friend, too, a man named Alex, and Lewis likes him. He brings presents sometimes, candy or a toy, and he likes to play catch in the backyard. Daddy doesn't smile anymore, and he's started drinking beer and stuff that smells like medicine but isn't medicine. Whenever Lewis visits the apartment, Daddy rarely takes him anywhere, and when he does, he's sullen and silent. Daddy doesn't have any friends, either. When Lewis asked him why, Daddy snapped, *Mind your own goddamn business, kid.* Lewis is now very careful about the kind of questions he asks Daddy.

The two of them sit quietly as the baseball game goes on. For reasons Lewis can't articulate, he's nervous. He senses something important depends on the game's outcome, but what it is, he doesn't know. The ninth inning comes, and the score is 7-8. It remains that way until the last few moments, when a batter hits a home run, and the game finishes 8-8. A tie.

Lewis looks at Daddy, and he's surprised to see his father smiling. It's small and more than a little sad, but it *is* a smile.

"There'll be another game," Daddy says. "Sooner or later."

Sometime while they were watching, Daddy picked up the shotgun and laid it across his lap. Now he strokes the metal barrel, almost caresses it, and Lewis shudders.

LEWIS STANDS IN FRONT OF THE PICTURE WINDOW IN his living room. The window is larger than the one in the dining room, and he has a better view of the Burns' house from here. He hears the shrill sound of a police siren cut through the air long before he sees the vehicle pull up in front of his house, lights flashing. The siren cuts off when the driver kills the engine, but the lights remain on. A pair of uniformed police officers get out of the vehicle, a man and a woman, both in their thirties. They take in the scene surrounding them – dead boy hanging from a tree, Clay's corpse lying broken and bloody in the street, the driver of the SUV who killed him lying several yards away, the top of her head blown off. Lewis is not surprised when the officers draw their weapons. He would do the same upon being confronted by this nightmarish tableau.

Tears of relief roll down his cheeks. The officers will deal with this madness now, and once he tells them what he saw, his part in it will be done. He has a bottle of whiskey in a kitchen cupboard, and after he gives his statement, he intends to spend the rest of the day emptying it.

He wipes the tears from his face with his hands, wipes his hands on his pants legs, then walks to the front door and steps out onto the porch. The officers haven't moved since getting out of their cruiser, and neither of them is looking in his direction. He calls out to them.

"Over here! I'm the one who called you!"

The officers spin around to face him, raise their guns, and fire.

A chunk of brick explodes on his right, and the glass of his storm door shatters behind him. Terrified, he ducks down and holds his hands out before him, palms up.

"Stop! I didn't do anything! I'm the one who called!"

He fears the officers will fire again, but they pause, look at each other, and then – somewhat reluctantly, he thinks – lower their guns. They don't holster their weapons, though. They walk toward Lewis' house and stop when they reach his porch steps, keeping their distance. He understands their caution. What if he *was* involved with the deaths somehow? They have no way of knowing he isn't dangerous.

He straightens and slowly lowers his hands, making sure to keep them in the officers' sight.

The man is tall and lean, with straight brown hair and a thin mustache. The woman is average height, with black curly hair and a round face. Both wear dark blue jackets with a police insignia on the left breast and dark blue pants. Their expressions are neutral as they approach, but Lewis can feel the intensity of their gazes on him. They're trying to determine if he's a threat, and given the scene that confronted them when they arrived, he can't blame them. He needs to assure them he's harmless.

"My name is Lewis Cooper. Like I said, I'm the one who called."

He tells them what happened, slowly at first, but once he gets started, the words pour out of him in a rush, as if he's purging himself of the horrible things he's seen. He expects the officers to interrupt to ask for clarification on certain points or maybe from disbelief that such bizarre circumstances actually happened. But the officers listen quietly, their expressions neutral. When he finishes, he waits for them to respond, but neither says anything right away. They exchange a quick glance, then turn to face him once more.

"Let me get this straight," the female officer says. "You called because you were concerned about the deaths you witnessed, right?"

No shit, Lewis thinks, but he nods.

The male speaks next. "And you *didn't* call because you yourself want to die."

For a moment, Lewis isn't sure he's heard correctly. "No."

The female again. "So you *weren't* looking to commit suicide by cop?"

Lewis' gut twists at her words. "Fuck no!"

The officers exchange another glance.

"We don't mind," the male says.

"We're happy to help," the female adds.

"It's our job to serve the citizens of this town," the male says.

"In whatever way they need," the female says.

Lewis can't believe what he's hearing.

"No reason to be ashamed about asking for help," the male says.

"Some have the constitution to do it themselves, but some need assistance," the female says. "Like the boy across the street."

The male smiles. "However we go, we all end up in the same place, and that's what really matters."

The female nods. "True."

They're just as crazy as the others, Lewis thinks.

How far has this madness spread? Throughout the entire town? Farther? And why isn't he?

"I . . . appreciate the offer, but I'm good for now. I'm, you know, working my way up to it."

Both officers nod.

"Perfectly understandable," the female says.

"We've been doing the same," the male says.

"But we're ready now, aren't we?"

"Yes, we are."

The two officers turn to face one another, raise their weapons until the barrels are pointed at each other's faces, and then fire.

Lewis screams.

"FUCK, FUCK, FUCK, FUCK, *FUCK!*"

Lewis stands in front of his TV, screen dark, remote gripped in trembling hand. He wants to turn the set on, tune in to a local channel, and see if there are any news reports about what's happening. Because *something* sure as shit is. Something *bad.* None of his neighbors have stepped outside to check on the cause of the gunfire, which they surely heard, and while his street is far from the busiest in town, aside from the woman who slammed her SUV into Clay, he hasn't seen a single vehicle pass by. He's witnessed five people die, all of them suicides – two assisted – and the police officers thought he called them to kill him. It's some kind of mass psychosis, a communicable darkness, just like . . . Memories threaten to rise, but he shoves them back down into the depths of his mind. He can't deal with them, not right now.

"Coward."

His father's voice, coming from behind him. So much has happened so fast that he's forgotten about seeing the ghost of his dead father in Clay's yard, the man's head ravaged by the shotgun blast that killed him. It was a hallucination brought on by the stress of the moment, that's all, and now it's back again. But it isn't *real*. It can't *hurt* him.

"Parents can always hurt their children, even when we're dead. Especially then."

Lewis squeezes his eyes shut. He isn't going to turn around, doesn't want to see.

"That's your problem, boy. You're an avoider. You're afraid to look reality straight in the eye and see it for what it is. You want to find out if everyone in town – maybe the whole goddamned world – is trying to off themselves? Then turn on the fucking news and look.*"*

Lewis opens his eyes, but he keeps his gaze fixed on the TV screen and concentrates on keeping his hand steady as he presses the remote's ON button. The system's menu comes up, and he scrolls through the channels until he finds MSNBC. He selects it and is rewarded with a panel of talking heads discussing the current state of the U.S. economy. He waits several moments to see if someone will cut in with a news bulletin about a rash of suicides occurring across the world, but when no one does, he switches to a local channel. He sees a silver-haired man and a younger woman slumped over a news desk. Both of their throats have been cut, and blood covers the desk's surface. The woman grips a box cutter in her right hand, and Lewis assumes she's cut the man's throat before slicing her own. There's no sound, and the image doesn't change. Lewis wonders if the staff are dead too. If the camera could somehow turn around on its own, would it show a scene of dead bodies sprawled across the studio floor? He thinks it might.

He begins to tremble again, but this time his entire body shakes. He tries another local station and gets a PLEASE STAND BY graphic, tries a third and sees a male reporter standing in front of a house with an elaborate Halloween display – realistic zombie mannequins in the yard, giant inflatable spider on the roof, twelve-foot skeleton standing next to the house, a life-sized coach harnessed to a black horse with glowing red eyes, inside a skeletal bride and groom, lipless teeth grinning, bony hands raised to wave a greeting to passersby. This latter decoration chills Lewis. Mr. and Mrs. Reaper, happy to share the gift of death wherever they go.

There's a sign in the yard that reads *Best Halloween Display*, with a gold ribbon attached to it.

"I'm Dale Morrison, signing off." The man grins. "Forever."

The man drops his mic to the ground before bending over to pick up a red plastic fuel container. He holds it over his head and pours liquid over himself. Once he's drenched, he throws the empty container aside, reaches into his jacket pocket, and pulls out a lighter. He thumbs a flame to life, touches it to his chest, and *whumpf,* his entire body is covered with fire. Lewis watches in horrified fascination as the man stands still and quiet as the flames eat away at his flesh. After a minute or so, the man begins convulsing, and then he falls to the sidewalk and lies there, a silent burning lump.

Lewis is trembling so hard now that it takes him three tries to turn off the TV. The screen finally goes dark, but in his mind, he still sees bright, flickering flame. So whatever is happening hasn't spread beyond town. That's something, at least.

"Hasn't spread yet," his father says.

Suddenly furious, Lewis spins around, intending to tell his father to go fuck himself, but the man isn't there. Lewis is relieved. While he isn't exactly thrilled to be hallucinating, it's far preferable to the alternative – that his father's ghost was actually here. But then he sees the dots of blood on the carpet where his father was standing. He takes a step forward, intending to touch a finger to the blood and see if it's real, but he stops himself. If he finds the blood tangible, then he'll have proof it – and by extension his father's specter – truly exists, and he can't handle that, not right now.

His father's words echo in his mind.

That's your problem, boy. You're an avoider. You're afraid to look reality straight in the eye and see it for what it is.

Maybe so. But whatever the hell is happening in this town, he can't hide or run from it. He's already involved – Clay, his grandson, the woman in the red pickup, the cops – and he fears it's going to get worse, maybe a *lot* worse. He has to do something, but he's not sure what he can . . . A single word flashes through his mind then, cutting like a razor through his thoughts.

Mom.

His sister Janice lives in San Francisco with her husband and two children, so they should be safe. But his mother still lives in town, and if any of her neighbors have killed themselves, it will be traumatic for her, given that his dad has taken his own life. And what if she's affected by the madness that's spreading through town? Is she still alive, or has she killed herself like Clay and the two officers?

He reaches for his front pants pocket, intending to pull out his phone and call his mother, but the pocket is empty. Where's his phone? Did he lose it? He remembers calling 911, and he hasn't left the house since, except to step onto his porch and talk to the officers when they arrived.

Did he drop it outside? He can't be without his phone, not now, not with everything that's happening. He's on the verge of panic when he remembers that he left his phone on the dining table next to his laptop. He rushes into the dining room, fearing that he's misremembered and his phone won't be on the dining table, but there it is, exactly where he left it. He realizes he's having trouble thinking straight – no surprise after what he experienced today – but he needs a clear head if he hopes to make it through this nightmare. He must try harder to focus on what's important and put everything else aside for now. He snatches the phone off the table and calls his mother.

One ring. Two. Three . . .

"Come on! Answer!"

Four rings. Five. . .

The call goes to voicemail.

"This is Claire. I'd love to talk with you, but I'm busy right now. Please leave a message, and I'll get back to you as soon as I can."

This is followed by a beep, and Lewis starts talking, an edge of hysteria in his voice.

"Mom, it's Lewis. Are you okay? There . . . There's something bad happening. People are dying, killing themselves, and I don't . . . I just want to make sure you're all right. Are you?"

A click as someone picks up.

"Mom? Is that you?"

No answer. Lewis thinks he can hear breathing on the other end, but he isn't certain. Then someone speaks, but it's not his mother. It's Dad.

"You better come over here, son. Things are really fucked up."

A click as his father disconnects. Lewis stands holding the phone to his ear for several seconds, breath caught in his throat. Then he runs into the kitchen, grabs his keys from a small metal dish on a counter, then races toward the garage, trying not to think about how bad the situation must be for the mutilated ghost of his father to consider them fucked up.

"Where are we going, Daddy?"

"Nowhere special. We're just taking a little trip."

Lewis is sitting in the passenger seat of his father's Camry, shivering. The heater's broken, and Daddy says he doesn't have the money to fix it. Lewis hopes he gets some money soon. It's early December, and winter is just getting started. He had a growth spurt over the summer and needs a new winter coat, but neither Daddy nor Mommy can afford it, so he has to make do with a lighter jacket. It's too tight, but it still kind of fits. The zipper's broken, though, and he has to hold it closed to keep out the cold. Before they left the apartment, he asked Daddy if he could bring a blanket to wrap himself in, but Daddy only said, *A real man doesn't let the weather get to him.* Lewis doesn't feel like a real man, though. He feels like a cold and miserable kid.

They did bring a blanket with them, but it's in the back seat, covering Daddy's shotgun. Daddy always takes it with him when he leaves the apartment, and while Lewis tries to pretend it's not there, he can't stop thinking about how cold the barrel would feel if he touched it, as if the weapon is made of ice instead of metal. He shivers even harder and looks out the passenger window, searching for something to distract him. It's only a little after six p.m., but it's already dark. Streetlights cast pools of fluorescence onto the road, and porchlights illuminate the fronts of houses they pass. The ground is bare – no snow yet this season – and Lewis thinks how much prettier everything would look if it were coated with white. It's easier to imagine the world is a better place when its ugliness is hidden.

"What the fuck?"

Lewis snaps his head around at Daddy's words, looks

out the windshield, sees a tortoiseshell cat sitting in the road, legs tucked beneath its body. It doesn't try to dart out of the way as the Camry's headlight beams wash over it, only turns its head to gaze upon the oncoming vehicle. Lewis presses his hands against the dashboard, bracing for impact, as if they're about to hit a brick wall instead of a small animal that's merely a collection of meat, bone, and fur. Lewis wants to shout, to warn Daddy about the cat, but everything is happening too fast, and the words won't come out. He hopes at the last instant the cat will realize the danger it's in, spring to its feet, and dart for safety. But it continues sitting there, unmoving, exuding a calmness that borders on serenity. A soft *whump*, a slight judder, and then they're past it.

Lewis fights an urge to turn around in his seat and look out the back window to check if the cat is still alive. He doesn't want to see its broken, mangled body, stomach burst open, internal organs spilled onto the road, asphalt around it stained crimson.

Daddy speaks then, voice soft.

"I couldn't avoid it. There was a car coming toward us in the other lane, and if I swerved to miss the cat, we would've hit it."

Us . . . We . . . As if Lewis shared responsibility for what had just happened. *He* wasn't the one driving, and *he* wasn't the one who didn't take his foot off the accelerator as they drew closer to the cat. He doesn't think

Daddy hit the animal on purpose, but Daddy didn't do anything to prevent it, either.

"Something was wrong with it," Daddy says. He grips the steering wheel tightly with both hands, his face pale. "Cats don't just sit in the road like that, not when there's a steady flow of traffic."

"Do you think it was sick?"

"Maybe. Probably. Could've been hit by somebody before us and gotten its brain scrambled. Wouldn't have had the sense to get out of the way then. Or it could've had cancer or something and wanted to die fast instead of slow." He pauses, then adds, "Everything that lives seeks death."

Lewis doesn't understand. "It was sitting the road because it wanted to kill itself?"

"How the fuck should I know? Do I look like an expert on cat behavior? Whatever caused that dumbass animal to lie down in the road, it's dead now, and there's no point in worrying over it. Best to put the incident out of your mind."

Lewis doesn't think he'll be able to do this, but he doesn't say this to Daddy. He thinks about the look in the cat's eyes right before they hit it. He'd never seen anything so at peace with itself, so *happy*.

They continue on in silence for a time. Residential neighborhoods give way to gas stations, fast-food restaurants, and check-cashing businesses, the buildings here old and shabby, the parking lots cracked and pot-holed, dead dry grass thrusting upward through the fissures. The streetlights are dim, and more than a few are burnt out. The shadows are thicker and darker here, and Lewis doesn't like it.

At times the car's engine sputters as it winds through the dark streets, and whenever it does, Daddy grits his teeth and says, "C'mon you bastard!" or "Don't you die on me, motherfucker!" Sometimes he slaps the dashboard when he says these things, as if he's threatening the car. *Do what I say or I'll hit you even harder.* Sometimes Daddy hits Lewis. Mommy too, but not often. Neither of them hit him before the divorce, but they both became meaner afterward, and he doesn't understand why. Sometimes he thinks they blame him for their divorce, but he doesn't remember doing anything to cause it. Maybe he did something without being aware of it, something *bad*. If so, he wishes his parents would tell him so he could try to make it right somehow. He would ask them, but they both get angry whenever he starts to talk about the divorce, and he's learned not to bring up the subject.

Lewis thinks of the happy look in the cat's eyes, and he wonders if the car would be happier if it stopped running and never turned on again. A car's life would be pretty boring, he thinks, if all it got to do was drive around town while its owner does stupid errands.

Where's the adventure in that, where's the *fun?* Cars can go anywhere as long as they have gas in their tanks and a smooth road to travel. They can go to the Grand Canyon or Hollywood or Alaska . . . Lewis would like to visit those places. He'd like to go anywhere that takes him away from the sad mess of his life.

Daddy slows, hits his left turn signal, pulls into a parking lot of a one-story building with a sign above the front door that says *Bear's Lair* in red letters, and *Products for Your Pleasure* in smaller letters beneath. Lewis has never seen this place before, and he's unsure what it is. A hunting store? Are there even bears in Ohio? He doesn't know. Maybe that's why Daddy bought the shotgun, because he plans to go hunting, and maybe he'll take Lewis with him. Lewis is both excited and scared by this prospect. He'd love to do something with Daddy since mostly they just hang around his apartment all the time, but he doesn't like the idea of killing any animal, especially bears. Cartoon bears always seem nice, but real bears are scary. They're big and strong and have sharp teeth and claws. Still, if Daddy asks him to go, he will. He wants to be a *real man*.

There are a handful of cars parked in front of the building, but Daddy doesn't join them. He drives past the Bear's Lair toward a nearby building that shares the same lot. This one's smaller, painted blue with white trim, a sign mounted on two poles driven into the ground near the road, white letters on blue background: *Club Elite.* Lewis isn't sure what *elite* means. Something that's fancy, he thinks, but there's nothing fancy about this place. The paint on the building is dull, faded, and flaking away, the windows are boarded over, and the asphalt in the parking lot is cracked and broken, large chunks of it missing, as if someone has carried them away for some unknown purpose. There's a single light in the lot, a pale yellow bulb attached near the top of a tall wooden pole, but otherwise, the area is cloaked in shadow. There are no cars parked here, but Lewis isn't surprised. The place looks like it's been abandoned for some time. Daddy stops the car next to the light, parks, and turns off the engine. He sits for a moment then, hands on the steering wheel, staring at the building, expression blank and unreadable. Finally, he turns to Lewis.

"I need to go inside for a while. I won't be gone long. I want you to stay here and wait. Don't get out of the car, and whatever you do, do *not* go any closer to the building. Do you understand?"

Lewis doesn't like the way the building makes him feel, and there's no way he'd ever go near it. He's uncomfortable with the idea of Daddy going inside, but Daddy's a grownup, so he must know what he's doing. Lewis nods.

Daddy turns and reaches into the backseat. For a

moment, Lewis thinks he's going to grab the shotgun, but while he does draw aside the blanket covering the weapon, he takes hold of several comic books that are sitting next to it. He hands them to Lewis, then pulls the blanket back over the gun.

"I got these for you so you'd have something to read while I'm gone."

There are three comics, and Lewis examines their covers. They aren't superhero comics – his favorites – but little kid comics featuring silly cartoon animals. Still, he's touched. Daddy doesn't usually get him presents.

Lewis smiles. "Thanks."

Daddy opens the car door, puts one foot on the ground, but before he completely exits the vehicle, he turns back to Lewis.

"Don't touch the gun."

Before Lewis can respond, Daddy gets out, swings the door shut, and starts walking toward the building with the flaking blue paint. Lewis watches him cross the parking lot, step up to the front door, open it, and disappear inside. He keeps watching for several more moments, as if he expects something to happen, although he's not sure what. Nothing does, though, and he turns his attention to one of the comics. The illumination provided by the light pole is feeble, but enough to see the pages by, even if it's a strain to make out the words in the characters' speech balloons.

This one features Dizzy Duck, a wise-cracking water-fowl who constantly plays tricks on the arrogant but not-too-smart Gary Gander in the forest pond where they live. As he reads, he tries to imagine that Dizzy is a superhero and Gary a villain, but it doesn't work. They're just stupid talking animals doing stupid things.

Forget that boring comic. Why don't you come back here and keep me company?

The voice is coming from the backseat.

From the gun.

Don't you want to know what my metal feels like beneath your fingers? Don't you want to take me in your hands, lift me up, feel how heavy I am, how real?

The shotgun's voice sounds like Daddy's, but tinny and hollow, as if Daddy is speaking to him from the far end of a long metal tube. Lewis knows he should be scared, but he tells himself that guns don't talk, he's just imagining this, and how can his own imagination hurt him?

"I guess so."

He puts the comic down and climbs into the backseat, careful to sit next to the shotgun, not on it. He reaches for the gun, but stops before he touches the blanket. He holds his trembling hand an inch above the fabric, not breathing, anticipating.

Come on, you little pussy. Shit or get off the pot.

Gently, almost reverently, he pulls the blanket aside, revealing the shotgun in all its glory.

He extends an index finger, presses it to the barrel, expects to find it cold, but it's warm, soft. Like flesh. He moves his finger back and forth, stroking it. It responds to his touch, growing warmer, firmer . . . Prompted by an instinct he doesn't understand, he wraps his fingers around the barrel, grips it tight, slides his hand up and down its length, slowly at first, then faster, faster . . .

Although Lewis' hand is nowhere near the trigger, the gun discharges loud as thunder, and projectiles blast into the door, tearing chunks out of the plastic. The gun recoils, the butt slams into his leg, and he cries out in pain. He sits there for several seconds, ears ringing, body shaking, tears running down his face.

Oh yeah, the shotgun says, its voice a purr. *That was so good . . .*

THREE WEEKS AFTER HIS DAD'S DEATH, LEWIS LIES IN bed, cover pulled up to his chin, hands gripping it tight as if he's afraid someone might try to yank it off him. It's late and his room is dark, so much so that he might as well be in a cave, miles beneath the earth's surface. His mother is still up, sitting at the kitchen table, glass in hand, bottle of scotch in front of her.

From the darkness, a voice – cold, contemptuous – whispers.

It's your fault.

It's his own voice, his father's, both.

If you'd been a better son, he wouldn't have done it.

You should've seen the signs, should've tried to stop him.

You're worthless.

"Shut up!"

He shouts these words – nearly screams them – and the horrible voice falls silent. Trembling, Lewis listens for several seconds, waiting for the voice to continue spewing its poison, but all he hears is the thudding of his heart and the rapid panting of his breath. Eventually, his pulse slows, as does his breathing, and a great weariness begins pulling him toward sleep. He settles against his pillow and closes his eyes. His body relaxes, and he feels a pleasant numbness spread through him as his consciousness starts to slip away. He has time for a final thought before he's gone.

Maybe I was asleep and only dreamed the voice.

It's a comforting lie – one he desperately needs right now – and he holds it close to his heart, like a toddler clinging to a beloved stuffed animal. And if he has any dreams, he doesn't remember them in the morning.

This is a blessing.

"THERE WAS ANOTHER ONE LAST NIGHT."

Lewis, fifteen, is looking down at his lunch when Shannon Armstrong says this – a rectangular slice of cheese pizza covered in grease, along with hard, dry peas and peaches slathered in syrup. *Today's lunch has been brought to you by the letter P*, he thinks. He has a small carton of chocolate milk to drink, and he thinks it's too bad the cafeteria doesn't serve soda, else he could've stuck with the P theme and gotten a Pepsi. He hasn't touched his food yet, and he doubts he will. He's not the only one without an appetite today. The cafeteria is half as full as it usually is – a lot of parents have been keeping their kids home the last few days – and the students who are present talk in hushed tones with each other or sit quietly, looking at their food like Lewis, but few are eating it. Shannon didn't bother buying lunch today, and Lewis wishes he did the same. The sight of it is making him queasy.

"Who was it?" he asks.

He doesn't really want to know, but this is the

response she expects from him, so he gives it. He still doesn't look at her, though.

"Mary Ellen Rinaldi." She pauses, as if expecting him to comment. When he doesn't, she goes on. "Her mom found her this morning in the bathtub, wrists slit and lying in a pool of blood. I guess she forgot to unplug the drain."

Lewis doesn't . . . *didn't* know Mary Ellen well. In one sense, he's known her most of his life, since this is a small town and they attended the same schools from elementary to middle school to high school, were in a number of the same classes. But he never spoke to her, at least not that he can recall, and he realizes that he has no memory of what her voice sounds . . . *sounded* like. So often people are like ghosts that haunt the edges of each other's lives.

Now he turns to Shannon—short red hair, green eyes, pale skin. She's smiling, but it's tentative, uncertain.

"Did she leave a note?" he asks.

"Not that I've heard, but none of the others did, so why would she?"

Mary Ellen is the fifth teenager in town to kill herself within the last seven weeks. None had any clear motive for ending their lives, at least that they'd shared with anyone, and they had no connection beyond going to the same school. It's like they had some kind of . . .

Disease, he thinks.

"Can you imagine what it must have been like for her mother to go into the bathroom and . . ." Shannon trails off, eyes widening. "Oh my god, Lewis, I'm so sorry, I wasn't thinking."

He sees his father sitting in his chair, most of his head gone, blood everywhere, shotgun still gripped in his dead hands.

"Not exactly a pretty sight, was it?"

He doesn't know if the voice belongs to the shotgun, his father, or both. He's not sure there's a difference.

Shannon lays a gentle hand on his shoulder.

"Lewis?"

He looks at her, but his mind is still focused on that awful scene from the past, and it takes several seconds before he registers her presence and remembers. They're in the cafeteria, and they're talking about Mary Ellen Rinaldi's suicide.

He manages a smile. "I'm okay. Just, you know, memories."

Her hand is still on his shoulder, but she removes it now and touches his cheek.

"I understand."

She slides her fingers up and down, caressing his skin. He wants to tell her to stop, but he remains silent and endures the contact. They met in art class last year and quickly became friends, but she considers them more than that, although the most they've ever done is hold hands. He hasn't liked to be touched by people, be *close* to them, since his dad's death. Shannon says she understands, but if she really does, then why is she touching him now? Perhaps she's not trying to comfort him so much as take comfort for herself. If that's the case, he's okay with it. Shannon's his friend, and he's willing to deal with some temporary discomfort if it helps her.

"She was in the same biology class as me," Shannon says. "I talked to her a few times. She was nice."

Ever since the first suicide –Vicky Wheeler, who'd choked herself by tying one of her father's ties to the knob of her bedroom door, wrapping it around her throat, then leaning forward – Shannon has become increasingly fascinated with the deaths. Lewis supposes it's only natural, morbid, but natural. Death is terror and mystery, and for someone to willingly embrace it earlier than they must is beyond comprehension for most.

He knows what Shannon is going to say next.

"Why do you think she did it? Why did *any* of them?"

He doesn't respond. Just because his dad killed himself doesn't mean he has any great insight into why someone would want to end their life. It seems like madness to him.

"You're a fine one to talk about madness."

The Daddy-Shotgun voice comes from somewhere behind him, but he ignores it. Shannon goes on.

"Sometimes I try to imagine what it must be like to feel so . . . so *hopeless*."

There's a hint of longing in Shannon's voice that Lewis doesn't like.

"Everyone feels hopeless sometimes," he says, "but it eventually goes away. You just need to hold on until it does. Nothing lasts forever."

"Death does," the voice says. *"Just ask them."*

Lewis doesn't want to turn around, and he wouldn't, except that the Daddy-Shotgun voice says *them*. He looks over his shoulder, sees his dead father standing next to one of the round cafeteria tables. The shotgun is cradled in his arms, and blood drips from the muzzle. Five teenagers sit at the table, all looking at Lewis and smiling. Vicky Wheeler, Kurt Massey, Roger Olson, Gordon Kim, and Mary Ellen Rinaldi – the five students who killed themselves. Vicky has a red ligature mark around her throat, and Mary Ellen holds a pair of blood-slick silver fabric scissors, skin pale from blood loss. Kurt doused himself with kerosene and set himself on fire, and now he's a smoldering, blackened husk with no discernible features. After saying goodbye to his parents, Roger drove his Camaro into a tree at eighty miles an hour, leaving him a bloody, broken mess. Gordon drowned himself in the backyard pool. His skin is wet and swollen, and reeks of chlorine.

Lewis doesn't take his gaze off the five – six, if you count his father – as he speaks to Shannon.

"It's okay. They're not real."

He hears the frown in her voice as she responds.

"Who isn't real?"

"Lunchtime!" his father says, and the five dead teenagers jump from their seats and race toward Lewis, hands outstretched and teeth bared. They grab hold of Lewis, drag him to the floor, and fall upon him like a pack of starving animals. He screams as they rip him open and pull out handfuls of gooey cheese, tomato sauce, peas, and peaches and jam the disgusting mess into their mouths.

His father laughs.

He fights the pain, closes his eyes, concentrates.

Not. Real.

The pain continues a moment more, and then all at once it's gone.

"You okay?"

He opens his eyes, sees Shannon looking at him, concerned. He quickly glances around, sees no sign of his father or of the kids who killed themselves. He releases a shaky breath and turns back to Shannon.

"Yeah . . . I think so."

But his father's laughter continues to ring in his ears.

LEWIS IS SITTING IN HIS PRIUS, HANDS GRIPPING THE steering wheel, knuckles white. He's driving too fast, and he thinks it would be ironic if he ends up wrecking his car and killing himself on the way to his mother's. His phone lies on the passenger seat, ringer on, in case she calls, but so far, it's been silent.

"You better come over here, son. Everything's really fucked up."

Images flash through his mind of his mother, each more disturbing than the last. Lying on the kitchen floor, throat sliced ear to ear, knife still in her hands. Thumbs jammed into her eye sockets, blood running down her face in crimson trails. A screwdriver penetrating one of her ears all the way to the handle.

"She'll be okay. She *has* to."

His mother lives on the other side of town, in an apartment building for senior citizens who don't yet need assisted living. Normally, he can get to her building in ten minutes, fifteen if there's heavy traffic. But today the streets are a war zone – multi-vehicle accidents, cars and trucks driven into light poles and buildings, metal crumpled and twisted, glass shattered . . . The people inside the vehicles, drivers and passengers alike, are broken and bloody, some dead, some dying, some badly wounded but still alive, moaning in agony, calling out for someone, anyone to please kill them. Even with his windows rolled up, Lewis can hear their pleas, and the longing in their voices, the *need*, makes him feel sick. Some of the survivors – ones whose bodies are still more or less intact and functional – have gotten out of their cars and now walk the road and sidewalks, expressions dull and dazed, bleeding from wounds on faces and scalps. Those not too wounded to run dash into the street as Lewis approaches, waving their arms and begging for him to run them down. He swerves to avoid them, but they throw themselves at his Prius, and he clips a few, injuring them further, but killing none. He winces with each *thud*, and by the time he enters his mother's neighborhood, he's crying.

LEWIS REMEMBERS ONE NIGHT WHEN HE WAS nineteen. He's taking classes at a local community college and still living with his mother, a cost-saving measure in preparation for his transferring to the University of Cincinnati the following year. He comes home from a study group around nine and finds his mother sitting at the kitchen table, a nearly empty bottle of scotch before her. Her glass is still half full, though, and when he walks into the kitchen, she holds it up to him in a kind of salute and downs the contents. She refills her glass, but she doesn't drink right away this time. She motions for him to sit, but he hesitates. Mom didn't drink alcohol much before the divorce, but afterward she started making up for lost time – especially after Dad's suicide. She usually has a buzz going when he gets home from class, and as the night progresses, she becomes thoroughly drunk. She gets talkative then, and Lewis ends up playing her audience and/or psychologist as she rambles on. He resents being forced into this role again tonight, but he sighs, sits, and waits for his mother to start talking.

Claire Cooper – she kept the surname after the divorce – is a tall brunette in her late fifties, but she looks ten years younger, maybe more. *All in the genes,* she says whenever anyone comments on how good she looks for her age. She's wrapped in a fuzzy blue robe, with matching slippers. There are dark splotches on the robe's fabric, places where she's spilled her drinks.

She picks up her glass, holds it to the light, and gazes at the amber-colored liquid inside.

"Sweet oblivion, Lewis. Nothing like it."

He thinks she'll gulp the scotch down and pour

herself another, but she takes only a small sip before looking at him.

"Your father was a fucking coward."

Her words hit him like a slap. He knows his mother didn't get along with his father – they only spoke when they had to, and never for long – but he's never heard such venom in her voice when she talks about him, no matter how drunk she becomes.

"I know our divorce hit him hard. It wasn't easy for me, either. But I took time to lick my wounds, and then I got back to the business of living. He was too afraid of confronting his pain, and in the end, that's why he killed himself."

Lewis' mother works as a business manager in an orthodontist's office, a job she's had ever since Lewis was a baby. So it isn't as if she needed to find new employment after the divorce. And he doesn't think that drinking yourself into a stupor every night counts as *living*. He doesn't say anything, though. When she gets like this, it's better not to interrupt and let her talk herself out.

"Suicide is a supremely selfish act. It's all about ending *your* pain, regardless of the consequences your death has on others. The way he traumatized you, allowing you to find him like that . . . Thank god I'm not that weak."

She finishes off her scotch in two quick gulps.

Yeah, Lewis thinks. *Thank god.*

THERE ARE SOME CRASHED VEHICLES IN HIS MOM'S neighborhood, but not as many as on the main roads. One of the houses is on fire, flames and dark smoke rising into the sky, and he wonders how many people are inside, fire devouring their flesh and blackening their bones. Someone who lives alone? A family? Or did a group of neighbors gather and throw a suicide party? Did they cheer as the first flames blossomed? Did they scream when the fire came for them or did they smile in beatific euphoria?

"What does it matter, as long as they got what they wanted in the end?"

His father's voice again. There's no one in the passenger seat, and when Lewis glances at his rearview mirror, he sees the back seat is empty. Good. As much as he hates hearing his father's voice in his head, it's better than seeing the physical manifestation of the man's mutilated body.

Lewis' anxiety spikes as he approaches his mother's apartment building, but from the outside, it appears as if everything is perfectly normal, no flames rising from the structure, no corpses lying on its lawn. It's a long one-story building at the end of a cul-de-sac, flat roof, square windows, a pair of glass-and-metal doors for the front entrance, old sycamore tree in the yard, neatly trimmed hedges against the outside wall. A place of bland functionality, a penultimate stop on the way to the end. Lewis pulls into the driveway and parks near the entrance. There are few cars here. The residents – those who have vehicles – park in a lot behind the building. Lewis grabs his phone and gets out of his Prius, but he doesn't bother locking the doors. There's nothing in the car worth stealing, and he has more important concerns right now.

He hurries through the front entrance. On the left is a counter where the building manager works, behind it a small office, but there's no one there. Whenever Lewis visits his mother, which isn't as often as he should, the building manager or one of his assistants is always standing at the counter to greet whoever enters. Not today, though. He knows it's a bad idea, but he can't keep himself from stopping and leaning over the counter to take a look. The manager is lying on the floor, forehead dented in, the skin there bruised and bloody. He sees a smear of blood on the counter, and he can guess what happened. The manager repeatedly slammed her head against the counter until she lost consciousness. Her ragged breathing tells Lewis she still lives, but for how much longer, he can't say. His phone is still in his hand,

and his instinct is to call 911, but he hesitates. He saw no sign of police or emergency vehicles out on the streets during the drive over. If he calls, will anyone answer, and if they do, will they send someone to save this woman's life or help her end it?

He slips the phone into his pants pocket.

The lobby leads to the main hallway, and Lewis steps into it and turns right. His mother's room is on the first floor, halfway down, on the left, Number 17. He starts walking, but soon he's running, and then he's standing in front of the door, breathing heavily, knocking.

"Mom? Are you there? It's me, Lewis!"

When there's no answer, he pounds his fist on the door.

"Mom!"

He's striking the door so hard now that his hand hurts, and he wonders if he's injured himself. He wishes he had a key to his mom's place, has asked her for one several times, but she's always refused. *I'm a grown-ass woman. I don't need you checking in on me whenever you start to worry. Besides, what if I've got a man with me? I may be old, but I'm not dead yet.*

He imagines his mother lying dead on the other side of the door, in her favorite chair, on her kitchen floor, in her bathtub, on her bed . . . Or maybe she's not dead, just badly injured, and she'll die soon if he can't get to her and help her. He tries kicking the door open, like he's seen characters in movies do, but either he's not strong enough or the movies are bullshit, because it doesn't work. If only he had a fucking *key!*

Maybe the manager has a pass key, one that allows him to unlock any door in the building. Given the residents' advanced age, he would need to let paramedics into apartments in case of a medical emergency.

Lewis runs back toward the lobby, hoping the manager has the pass key in one of his pockets, but halfway there, he hears a sound and stops to listen. Music, faint, but unmistakable. Something classical, but he doesn't recognize the composer. Mozart? Hayden? One of those guys. It's coming from farther down the hallway, past the lobby.

From the common room.

He starts running again.

While this isn't an assisted-living facility, it does have a place where residents can meet to have meals together, share a cup of coffee, watch TV on a big screen, or simply chat. There's regularly scheduled activities too, crafts, sing-alongs, game nights . . . As he runs, he hears a man's voice call out over the music –

"I-6!"

– followed by a woman's voice.

"Bingo!"

Applause and scattered groans.

The double doors to the common area are open, and

when he reaches the entrance, he rushes inside – and stops. Men and women, silver-haired, wrinkled, stooped, sit at round tables, bingo cards spread out before them. A man stands at the far end of the room, next to a tabletop bingo cage filled with numbered white balls. This is Lewis' dead father. Next to him is another round table at which no one is sitting. On its surface rests Dad's shotgun and several boxes of shells, alongside a paper cutter, the kind with a base and a long scythe-like arm. There's blood on the cutter's blade and surface – a lot of it – and it's running off and pattering to the tiled floor to join a large pool of the red stuff there. The floor beneath and around the table is thick with crimson, and a half dozen severed hands lie in the gore. A few feet away, six old people – four women and two men – sit with their backs against the wall. Each is missing a hand, and blood flows from the ragged stumps of their wrists. Their eyes are closed, and Lewis can't tell whether they're alive or dead.

As he stands there, stunned by the scene before him, an elderly woman rises from her table, bingo board in hand, and starts walking toward Lewis' dad. Her head is lowered, her back hunched – she has severe osteoporosis, Lewis guesses – but she moves easily enough. When she reaches Dad, she hands him her board, and he holds it to his shotgun-ravaged face. He doesn't have eyes anymore, but he nevertheless examines the board. The players have been using erasable markers to keep track of the numbers that have been called. The marker color? Red, of course.

Dad holds the card up high. *"We have a winner!"* he shouts, blood spraying from his ruin of a mouth.

The woman grins and steps over to the table with the shotgun and the paper cutter. The residents applaud, holler, whistle, stamp their feet, and Lewis spots his mother. She's sitting at a table near the back of the room, and she's grinning and clapping along with everyone else, a strange gleam in her eyes, an expression of almost fevered anticipation on her face. Of all the horrible things Lewis has seen today, his mother's eager bloodlust is the worst.

Lewis enters the common room and walks quickly toward the table with the paper cutter. He does this without any conscious decision on his part, his body acting on its own. He's witnessed too much death this day and can't bear to witness any more. The woman at table places her left hand on the cutting board's blood-slick surface then grips the blade's handle.

"No! Stop!" Lewis shouts.

But as he passes in front of his father, the dead man unlatches the hopper's door and gives the hopper a spin. White balls with letters and numbers on their surfaces – far more than the small bingo cage should be able to hold – shoot out, hit the floor, bounce, and roll. Lewis tries to avoid stepping on them, but there are too many, and his feet fly out from under him, and he falls to the floor, landing hard on his back. He struggles to rise, but the impact has knocked the breath out of him, and all he can do is gasp for air and watch as the old woman brings the cutting board's blade down on her wrist. There's a loud *ka-chunk*, blood sprays, and the crowd cheers wildly, like spectators at a football game when a touchdown has been scored. The woman picks up her severed hand and holds it high for everyone to see, then she drops it onto the floor with the others, and steps over to where the previous "winners" are sitting, blood spurting from the stump of her left hand and adding to the crimson mess on the floor. Blood loss is already affecting her, and she's staggering by the time she reaches the others. She turns, presses her back against the wall, and instead of slowly lowering herself to the floor, she lets herself fall. She sits there, smile on her face, dull look in her eyes, blood pooling on the floor around her.

Lewis manages to prop himself up on one elbow. It's still a struggle to breathe, but it's getting easier.

"Sorry about that," his father says, *"but I couldn't let you interfere with her godgiven right to end her life in a manner of her choosing. We have no choice when it comes to being born, but we have a choice about how we shuffle off this mortal coil – if we're strong enough to take it."*

Lewis rises to his feet, careful not to step on any more bingo balls, then turns to look at his father.

"I don't give a damn about your bullshit nihilism. I'm not sure you're actually real. Hell, I'm not sure *any* of this is." He makes a sweeping gesture to indicate the one-handed senior citizens sitting against the wall and the audience of their peers. "I came here to get Mom and take her someplace safe. Once we leave, you can all go back to playing mutilation bingo. But we're leaving."

"It's not your choice to make, Lewis."

He turns and sees his mother standing close by. She grins.

"So stay the fuck out of it."

The remaining seniors stand now, gazes dark, features twisted in anger, hands curled into fists.

You want to get your mom out of here? I can help.

Lewis recognizes the voice in his head. It's the shotgun.

He looks at the weapon lying on the paper cutter table, the underside of its stock and barrel coated with blood. It would be slick in his grip, but he thinks he'll be able to hold it well enough.

I'm the solution to all your problems, Lewis. The final solution.

The shotgun's cold laughter echoes through his mind. He glances at his father, wonders if he hears the shotgun's voice too, but it's impossible the read the emotions of a man with no features. Lewis gauges the distance between himself and the gun, and he's confident he can reach it before anyone can stop him. He's young, and Mom and the other residents are old. He's faster than them, stronger too. He's never held a gun of any type before – after finding Dad's body, the thought of merely touching one makes him nauseous – let alone firing one, but how hard can it be? Just aim and squeeze the trigger. He can do this, *has* to do this.

But before he can take more than a single step, his mother lets out a shriek and rushes toward him. A split second later, the other residents do the same. Lewis runs for the table, stretches out his right hand, lunges for the shotgun . . .

Then something hard slams into the back of his head, there's an explosion of pain, and he tumbles down into darkness.

AS AN UNDERGRAD, LEWIS GOES THROUGH A PHASE where he tells bad jokes about suicide.

"The more suicidal people there are, the less suicidal people there are."

"Suicide is never the answer. Suicide is the question. The answer is yes."

"Where do suicide bombers go when they die? Everywhere!"

"Why did the chicken commit suicide? To get to the Other Side."

"You call it suicide. I call it a failed parkour attempt."

"What's the worst advice you can give to a suicidal person? Hang in there!"

"What's the difference between a bridge and a burrito? I can't jump off a burrito."

"I went to the morgue and asked if they took walk-ins."

Some people laugh – often uncomfortably – some look at him with shock or disgust, and some simply walk away. Once in the campus coffee shop, he talks too loudly while telling a suicide joke to one of the few friends who still hang around him, and a girl at the next table gets out of her seat and comes over to confront him.

"My older brother killed himself last year. In the middle of the night, while the rest of us were asleep, he went into the garage, put a rubber hose in the tailpipe of my parents' car, stuck it through a crack in the driver's side window, and turned on the engine. We didn't find him until morning. You wouldn't make jokes about suicide if you knew someone who actually fucking did it."

Her cheeks are flushed with anger, but her tone is icy calm. Lewis wants to tell her he does know someone who killed themselves, and that's precisely *why* he makes these jokes. But there are tears brimming in her eyes, and instead of defending himself, he says, "You're right. I'm sorry."

She looks at him a moment longer, then turns away and goes back to her table. Some of the people seated nearby overheard their exchange, and they look at him now. Their faces are gone, teeth shattered, meat red and raw, and there are shotgun muzzles where their eyes used to be. Voices come from the ruins of their mouths, and they say, *You're worthless*.

He looks down at the table, whispers, "I know."

LEWIS IS TWENTY-SIX BEFORE HE LOSES HIS virginity.

He's in the first year of his doctoral program at the University of Cincinnati when he meets Rene Bryant at a friend's New Year's Eve party. She's a petite brunette working on a Master's in Music Therapy, and since neither of them came with dates, they spend most of the night together, talking and laughing, and at midnight, they're both surprised to find themselves sharing the traditional kiss.

They begin dating, and Rene – who is an open, expressive person – attempts to introduce sex into their burgeoning relationship within the first week. She's good at reading signals, though, and when she senses his reluctance, she takes things slowly, and soon they're making each other cum with hands and mouths, which is as far as Lewis is comfortable going, and for a while, Rene contents herself with this. But eventually she becomes frustrated, not with the sex itself, but with the lack of progress on the emotional side of things. She tells him this, and after a moment, Lewis tells her about his dad's suicide and the effect it's had on his ability to open up emotionally to others.

When he finishes, she says, "I'm so, so sorry."

They're lying in her bed, naked, sheet tossed onto the floor because the room is too warm. She cups his cheek in her hand, leans over, kisses him lightly. She draws away then, but he puts his hand on the back of her head, pulls her toward him, and kisses her deeply. Things flow naturally after that, and Lewis is surprised at how easily he gives himself to her and at the sheer joy he feels in the giving. He's not aware of the exact moment he enters her, but soon they're moving together, in total sync, unclear where one starts and the other begins. It's the happiest he's ever been in his life, and if he could preserve this moment and live within it for eternity, he'd do so. His climax comes upon him in a sudden rush; he tries to stop it, fails, and he explodes within her.

Like a shotgun.

The sound is deafening.

Still inside her, he squeezes his eyes shut tight.

He opens his eyes, sees the top of her skull is gone, sees red smeared across the headboard, sees her blood soaking the pillow beneath her. Her eyes are staring and glassy, her mouth open, but from somewhere inside her comes a voice.

Don't be embarrassed, love. It happens to everyone sometimes.

This isn't real! It can't be!

"Did you hear me? I said it's okay. Really!"

Renee is alive and unharmed, the blood gone.

Lewis rolls off her and starts to cry. After a moment, she rolls over, wraps her arms around him, and holds him tight.

IN THE DARKNESS, LEWIS BECOMES AWARE OF

classical music playing softly. He thinks it's Camille Saint-Saëns' "Dance of the Animals," but he's not sure.

He opens his eyes.

He's lying on his right side, head pounding like a motherfucker, neck and upper shoulders aflame. Someone hit him from behind, but he's not sure with what. Most likely one of the metal folding chairs everyone was sitting in. He sits up, and immediately regrets it as a wave of nausea hits him. He thinks he's going to throw up, but he doesn't, and after several seconds, the nausea subsides, although it doesn't go away entirely. He wonders if he has a concussion. Should he go to the ER? But then he remembers exactly where he is and what was happening before he lost consciousness, and all thought of his injuries and how severe they might be vanishes. He stands on shaky legs, looks around the room, neck screaming with pain as he turns his head back and forth. The common room has become a slaughterhouse, bodies of old people lying everywhere, some missing hands, others with faces and heads nothing but mangled meat, shattered bone, and everywhere there's blood, so much blood . . . The shotgun still lies on the table where he last saw it, empty cardboard boxes that once held shells lying on the floor around it. Only one box remains on the table, but from where he stands, he can't tell if it holds any shells. The sight of a folded chair lying on the floor close by confirms his theory of how he was attacked. He wonders if his mom did it.

He sees no sign of his dad, thank Christ, and while it's not easy to tell given the state of some of the corpses' faces, it doesn't look like his mom is here either. He doesn't know whether or not to be relieved by this. He walks over to the shotgun, checks the box of shells, sees a few remain, scoops them up, and tucks them into his front pants pocket. He sees something else on the table then, a small white rectangular object, and he realizes it's a matchbook. He can read the words on the cover just fine, but he still picks it up and holds it closer to his face, as if he wants to make sure it's real.

Club Elite.

He stares at it for several moments before sliding it into his pocket to join the shells.

Ready to go? the shotgun asks.

"As I'll ever be."

He picks up the gun, holds it down at his right side, and heads toward the hallway.

HE PULLS INTO THE SAME SPACE WHERE HIS DAD parked so many years ago, turns off the engine, and sits for a moment. He's actively avoided this part of town since the day Dad brought him here, and it's his first time seeing Club Elite in decades. It's late afternoon now, the sky clear and gray, night not far off. The building is older and more weathered than when he last saw it, only a few stubborn flakes of paint left on its façade, the parking lot spiderwebbed with so many fissures, it seems like a strong wind could blow the fragments away, revealing the dead dry earth beneath. There are no other cars in the lot, but Lewis knows this doesn't mean the building is empty. He grabs the shotgun – which was mercifully silent on the drive here – and gets out of his car.

The trip from his mom's building was as nightmarish as the trip there, wrecked vehicles in the streets, dead bodies scattered on sidewalks, lawns, and in parking lots, with who knew how many more concealed inside the various structures he passed. Is there anyone still alive in town besides him? Maybe not, and depending on how the next few moments go, he might not be around much longer himself.

What is it about this place that drew his father here, what *need* in him did it satisfy? He supposes he's about to find out.

He starts walking toward the building's entrance.

Lewis regularly discusses the topic of suicide with his classes.

From a sociological perspective, societal and cultural stressors are as much a cause of suicide as individual ones, if not more so. Individual stressors may increase the potential for suicide in some members of a society, but large-scale stressors can increase the potential for suicide in all members.

"I don't want to see you anymore."

Lewis was about to eat another bite of his crab alfredo, but he pauses, the fork halfway to his mouth. He looks at the woman sitting across from him – a tall redhead with fair skin, hands resting on the table's surface, one over the other. She's sitting straight, her demeanor serious, as if she's about to deliver an Important Lecture to a class. He hasn't realized it until now, but she's barely touched her mahi mahi.

Flora McLaughlin teaches at the same college as Lewis, although not in the Sociology department. She's a Psychology professor, well-liked by everyone – students, faculty, and administrators. She and Lewis have been dating for almost two months, and up to this moment, he thought things were going well between them. Evidently not.

Lewis puts down his fork.

"You mean you want me to be invisible?"

It's a terrible joke, but she caught him off guard, and it's all he can think to say.

She doesn't come close to cracking a smile.

"Honestly, in some ways, you already are."

"I don't –"

She raises a hand to cut him off.

"You're not emotionally available."

He frowns. "I don't know what that means."

"You must have some idea. Sociology and psychology overlap to a certain degree, the study of people and all that."

Yep. Definitely lecture mode.

"Sorry. Guess I slept through that class."

She gives him a thin smile.

"You have trouble connecting with people, Lewis. Your emotional barriers are so strong no one can get through, and you never let anyone in. Not even someone you've been physically intimate with."

Lewis takes a quick look around to see if any of the diners near them are listening, but everyone seems focused on their own meals and conversations.

"Let me ask you a question, Lewis."

He wishes she'd stop saying his name like that, dropping it in at the end of sentences as if he's a distractible child and she wants to ensure he's paying attention.

"Go on."

"How did you feel when I said I didn't want to see you anymore?"

He opens his mouth to answer, but he pauses, unsure of what to say. What the hell *did* he feel?

"I was surprised. I thought things were going well between us."

Her smile is sardonic. "Of course you did. What else did you feel?"

He's starting to get angry now. "Are you going to bill me for a therapy session when we're done talking?"

"Please. Humor me."

Lewis wants to tell her to go to hell, but he really likes her. He thinks for a moment, then shakes his head.

"Sorry. Surprised is all I got."

Flora nods, as if he's given the answer she expected.

"You weren't upset? Sad, angry, scared to lose me?"

"You caught me off guard. I haven't had time to have any feelings yet."

"You didn't have any reaction because you haven't

allowed any sort of emotional connection to develop between us. We aren't really lovers. Hell, we're not even really friends."

Lewis wants to deny this, but he knows it's true. He should say something, though, maybe apologize to her, but he's unsure how to go about it. Flora takes his silence for permission to continue talking.

"I don't want you to feel bad, Lewis. Your resistance to emotional involvement is perfectly understandable given what your father did. It traumatized you deeply. How could it not?"

Lewis' jaw muscles tighten, and his hands curl into fists. He removes his hands from the table, lower them so Flora doesn't see how upset he's become, but her eyes track the movement, and a small smile plays around her lips. She's enjoying this, he realizes, likes seeing his control slip, if only a little.

"But just because I empathize with your issue doesn't mean I don't have needs of my own. I need emotional intimacy in a romantic relationship as well as physical. I need to feel *connected* to my partner. And you're not capable of that, Lewis. Not right now, anyway, but with time and the right therapy, who knows? Regardless, you and I are not going to work out. I'm sorry."

He should've seen this coming. The few times he's allowed himself to pursue a relationship, they've always ended like this, with the woman telling him he was starving her emotionally.

"You mentioned my *issue*. Is that why you went out with me in the first place? Because you wanted to get a peek at the inner workings of someone as fucked-up as I am? Conduct a little psychological voyeurism? Maybe indulge a bit of messiah complex and try to be the one to finally fix me?"

Flora's cheeks redden in shame or anger, maybe a mix of both.

Lewis continues.

"It must be infuriating that with all your education and professional experience, you couldn't put my pieces together again. Like Oscar Wilde said, 'We are each our own devil, and we make this world our hell.' But if you want to get into my mind so badly, I can help you out."

Lewis stands, reaches up, puts both hands on his head, digs his fingers into his scalp, and *pulls*. There's a wet, sticky sound as he tears away two flaps of hair and skin and drops them to the floor. Flora watches, wide-eyed, face pale, as he jams blood-slick fingers into his skull, pries off chunks of bone, exposes his brain to the open air. He discards the bone fragments, jams his right hand into the opening, and pulls forth a bloody mass of brain tissue.

"Bon appétit!" he shouts, then lunges forward and

shoves the meat into Flora's mouth, quite literally giving her a piece of his mind.

No! No, no, no, NO!

He blinks. He's sitting at the table, Flora across from him, looking at him quizzically. He gives her a thin, weary smile.

"Sorry, but I've lost my appetite."

He rises and slowly walks away.

LEWIS STEPS UP TO CLUB ELITE'S ENTRANCE, HIS head and neck still throbbing from being hit with the chair at his mom's building. Since he's holding the shotgun in his right hand, he grasps the doorknob with his left, turns it. He's not surprised to find the door unlocked. He's been invited, after all. He pushes the door open, steps inside. He doesn't close it behind him, though. He may need to leave in a hurry – assuming he survives. The windows are boarded up and it's dark in the building, but the light coming in through the open doorway allows him to see well enough, and what he sees is a small lounge area: bar, tables, chairs, concrete floor, no decorations on the walls, everything covered in a thick layer of dust. The dust is undisturbed, but Lewis knows he's not alone in this place. He shifts the shotgun to a two-handed grip as he moves deeper into the building.

It's spooky in here, isn't it?

It's the first thing the gun has said since Lewis picked it up back at his mom's building, and it's not wrong. The minimal furnishings make the place seem like the skeletal remains of a lounge rather than a lounge itself, and there's a cold sterility in the air, like you might find in a hospital –

Or a morgue?

Yes.

Lewis tries to imagine people here once, talking, laughing, drinking – his dad among them – but this doesn't feel like a place where people gathered for companionship. This was a place where they waited, in silence and anticipation, until . . . what?

To the right side of the bar is a doorway covered by a black curtain.

To go through there, he thinks.

The lounge area is small, and the building – while not huge – is larger than this. He makes his way past the few tables and chairs, and when he reaches the curtain, he uses the shotgun's barrel to draw it aside.

Now the fun really *begins!* the shotgun says.

Lewis knows there's no point in telling it to shut up. Whether the voice is real or only in his mind, it'll say what it wants when it wants.

He steps through the doorway and into a narrow hall-way. As in the lounge, the walls are unadorned, the floor concrete, but the air is colder here, making it feel as if it's the dead of winter instead of early October. There's no source of light here, and it's difficult to make anything out in the gloom. He stops for a moment, gives his eyes time to adjust, and soon he can see that several rooms branch off the hallway, three on each side, their doors open. He starts forward, moving cautiously. The rooms are opposite each other, and when he reaches the first pair, he looks right, then left, shotgun gripped tight, finger on the trigger. More minimal furnishings, this time soiled mattresses, small rectangular tables, and metal buckets sitting on the floor.

Those are for catching the blood, the gun says.

Images flash through Lewis' mind – naked men and women, some with silk ropes wrapped around the throats, smiling beatifically as someone equally naked strangles them, others sitting cross-legged on the floor, arms stretched out over buckets, while someone else slowly, lovingly, parts their flesh with a straight razor. He can hear the metallic patter as the blood hits the bottom of the buckets, the sound like thick, heavy rain. Was this some kind of suicide club?

Yes and no, the shotgun says, sounding amused. *You'll see.*

Lewis gives his head a hard shake to dispel the visions, then continues walking to the end of the hallway. Another doorway here, another black curtain. He opens it as he did the first, steps through, and finds himself in utter darkness. It's even colder in here, and he starts to shiver. He has a sense of space all around him, but he can't see a goddamned thing.

"Is anyone here?" he calls out. His voice echoes, confirming his impression of the room's size.

His dad replies.

"Everyone's here!"

Light flares to life, bright and blinding, and Lewis shuts his eyes and turns his head. After a moment, he slowly opens his eyes and turns back to see what the light has revealed. It's a meeting room of some sort, like the common area at his mom's building, only not as large, and instead of plaster, wood, or tile, the walls, floor, and ceiling are made of a red, wet substance that he can't identify at first. A coppery tang hangs in the air, thick and greasy, and he realizes that what he's smelling is blood, and then he understands what the room is formed from – great slabs of raw, glistening meat. In the middle of the ceiling is a large orb that can only be an eye, and it blazes with a sour, yellow light, illuminating the room. There are no tables, but a single wooden chair is positioned near the back wall, and a child sits upon it, a child that Lewis recognizes. Dozens of naked people fill the meat-room, huddled together to leave an open passage to the chair and the child sitting on it. Lewis' mother stands to the right of the chair, his father on its left, both unclothed like the others, his features ravaged by the shotgun blast that killed him, his mother missing her right hand, skin pale from blood loss. Lewis knows then that he's arrived too late to save her.

He recognizes the others gathered here as well, like his parents, their flesh marked by the physical signs of their deaths. Shannon from high school, along with the five students who killed themselves back then –Vicky

Wheeler, Kurt Massey, Roger Olson, Gordon Kim, and Mary Ellen Rinaldi. The girl from the college coffee shop who was offended by his tasteless suicide jokes. Rene Bryant, the music therapy major he had sex with in grad school. Flora the psychology professor from his college. The local newscasters he saw kill themselves on television. The old people and the site manager from his mom's building. The two cops who responded when he called 911, the woman who drove the red pick-up truck, and of course, Clay Burns and his grandson, the two who started this madness for Lewis earlier that day. They're all smiling, gazing upon him with fascinated adoration.

His father motions for him to come forward.

"Come closer. He won't bite."

"Not yet, anyway," his mother adds.

His parents laugh, and the onlookers join in. Lewis doesn't want to go forward, doesn't want to step onto the soft red floor, would rather turn around, get the fuck out of there as fast as he can, and pretend that none of this ever happened. But he came here to understand what the hell is going on in this town, and what, if anything, can be done to stop it. He steps forward, the meat-floor bowing sickeningly beneath his weight, and he walks toward his parents and the child on the chair, feeling absurdly like he's walking down the aisle at a wedding, or perhaps approaching a coffin at a viewing.

Why not both? the shotgun says.

The crowd begins chanting softly now, a single word, repeated over and over.

Worthless, worthless, worthless . . .

Lewis stops six feet from the child on the chair and examines him closely. It's him, of course, or at least a version of him, seven years old, the same age he was when his father killed himself. The boy is naked like all the others, but unlike them, his flesh is unmarred and a healthy pink. He's alive, or at least he looks that way. His features are slack, his eyes don't blink, and his chest doesn't rise and fall.

"He's not quite ready yet," his dad says. *"There's one thing missing."*

His mother grins with what's left of her mouth. *"A very special ingredient."*

They're talking about you, the shotgun says.

"I figured." He looks at his parents. "What *is* this place? More importantly, what is that *thing?*" He nods toward his younger doppelganger.

The crowd's combined voices are like dark ocean waves breaking against a hard, obsidian shore.

Worthless, worthless, worthless . . .

"The sign outside says Club Elite," his mom says. *"But its real name is the Shrine of the Meat Sacrament."*

"You already know these things," his dad says. *"You just need reminding."*

Young Lewis moves for the first time since Older

Lewis entered the room. He stands, takes three quick steps, stretches out his right hand, and touches the tip of his index finger to Lewis' forehead. Images and sounds explode in his mind, and he feels himself falling down through the years.

"– OUT WITH HIS *FRIENDS* AGAIN. FUCKING FREAKS."

Lewis is six. He's supposed to be in bed, and he *was*, was even *asleep*, but he heard his mother talking loudly, and it woke him. He snuck down the hallway from his bedroom to peek into the kitchen, hoping to find his father is home, but Mommy sits alone, unless you count a three-quarters empty bottle of scotch and a shot glass. She downs the drink as easily as if it's water, pours herself another. She keeps her fingers on the glass, but she doesn't immediately lift it off the table.

"I told him it was all bullshit, no different than any other church. Fools who think they can get special shit from their god, priests only too happy to take advantage of them . . ." She shakes her head. "I thought you were smarter than that, Bob. Guess I was wrong."

She throws the drink back, slams the glass on the table, but this time she makes no move to refill it.

"Fuck it."

She knocks the shot glass over, grabs the scotch bottle by the neck, and rises to her feet. She stands there a moment, swaying slightly, and Lewis fears she's going to fall over – he's seen it happen before when she's been drinking. But she manages to stay upright, and she starts walking away from the table. Toward Lewis.

He turns, hurries down the hallway, walking on the balls of his feet to make as little sound as possible. He slides into his room, pulls the door most of the way shut – doesn't want Mommy to hear the *click* of him closing it – gets into bed and burrows under his covers. Mommy has never hurt him before, so he's not afraid she will hit him or spank him, but she *will* yell at him if she thinks he was out of bed, and he doesn't want that. Plus, he senses there's something different about tonight. He witnessed what was supposed to be a private moment – like accidentally seeing one of your parents naked – and if Mommy knows he heard what she said, she'll be angry, sure, but she'll also be embarrassed, and he can't stand the idea of making her feel like that.

He listens as she comes clomping down the hall. She pauses at his door, and he wonders if she notices that it's open a crack. Will she come in and yell at him for getting up on spying on her? Nothing happens for several long moments, then Mommy gently pulls the door shut and continues down the hallway to the bedroom she shares with Daddy. When he hears her open and close the door, he exhales with relief. He closes his eyes, tries to go back to sleep, but he can't stop wondering why Mommy thinks there's something wrong with Daddy's friends.

WORTHLESS, WORTHLESS, WORTHLESS . . .

DADDY'S BIG HAND ON HIS SHOULDER IN THE DARK, flesh warm, grip light but firm, the smell of adult sweat only barely masked by deodorant. They walk past closed doors. Sounds come from behind them, muffled cries of pain or pleasure, Lewis can't tell which. They make his stomach feel funny, but in a way that's not altogether unpleasant.

"What are they doing?" he asks in a whisper.

"Worshipping," Daddy says.

Lewis doesn't understand, but after what happened in the parking lot, he's too afraid to ask any more questions. When Daddy came out of the blue building and saw what

Lewis had done with the shotgun, he was sure he was in bad trouble. But to his surprise, Daddy smiled and asked him if he heard the gun talk. When he said yes, Daddy smiled and said, *"You're ready."* He led him into the blue building and now they approach a second curtained-off doorway. Daddy carries a penlight, and Lewis sees him draw the curtain aside. He hears the soft sound of sliding cloth, and then Daddy ushers him into the room beyond.

It's dark in here, like the hallway, but bigger, and it smells funny. The floor is soft, kind of like in a bouncy castle, but more solid.

They stop, and Daddy says, "There's someone I want you to meet."

He sounds proud, but scared as well, as if he's unsure what will happen next. Lewis has never known Daddy be afraid before, and this makes him scared too. Daddy swings the beam of his penlight slowly back and forth, as if looking for something, but there's nothing there. The walls, ceiling, and floor are red and moist, striated with white lines. Dad pan-fried steaks for dinner the weekend before, and the room reminds him of what the meat looked like before it was cooked. The thought makes him feel queasy, and he's afraid he might throw up.

Dad speaks again, louder this time.

"I've come to present my son to you, Lord. Will you grace us with your presence?"

No one answers, but Lewis thinks he sees movement in one of the room's corners. The shadows are darker there, and they seem to surge and roll, like waves from a vast dark sea. Then the darkness is racing toward him, engulfing him in its cold embrace. He opens his mouth to scream, but the darkness rushes into him, choking off his voice. As if from a great distance, he hears Daddy speak, his words faint, barely audible.

"Lewis, meet the Unhigh."

Then, so softly Lewis isn't sure he hears it at all, Daddy adds, "I'm so proud of you."

The darkness fills him entirely then, and for a long time, he knows nothing else.

WORTHLESS, WORTHLESS, WORTHLESS . . .

"YOU KNOW WHAT I HEARD?"

Lewis and Shannon are walking down the high school's first-floor hallway, on the way to their morning advisory. Lewis has a midterm in American History today, and he didn't study for it as well as he should have, and he's worried he's going to bomb it. So he's only half paying attention to what Shannon is saying.

"What?" he asks.

"That all of their parents belong to that same weird club your dad did."

That got his attention.

"Who?"

"You know – Kurt, Vicky, Roger, Mary Ellen, and Gordon. Their parents are all members of Club Elite. What the hell *is* that place?"

Lewis starts to answer, but his mind is a sudden blank on the subject. He often has trouble remembering things about Club Elite, sometimes even forgetting the fact that it exists at all. His dad went there regularly before he died, and his mom always resented him for it, thought it was a stupid waste of time. Lewis went there too, he thinks, at least once. He isn't sure.

"I don't know," he says. "I really don't."

WORTHLESS, WORTHLESS, WORTHLESS . . .

LEWIS WAKES ON THE FIRST SATURDAY IN OCTOBER, head pounding, throat and mouth dry, stomach aching. In his recycling bin in the kitchen are two empty bottles of bourbon. He only intended to drink part of one last night, but one thing led to another, as it usually does when he drinks, and so he cracked the second bottle. He hates it when he loses control like that. It reminds him too much of his mother. At least he didn't open the *third* bottle – that one's still in the cupboard.

He went on a date last night, one arranged through a popular app, but the woman and he couldn't have been more mismatched. She's a narcissist who talked about herself all evening without asking him a single question about himself. She works at the corporate headquarters for a banking chain, and all she cares about is money – primarily making it for herself. They ate dinner at a Thai place, one of Lewis' favorites, and halfway through the meal, the woman spotted someone she knew at another table and hurried over to talk to them. She stayed there for almost half an hour, more than enough time for Lewis to finish his Panang curry as well as order and eat some mango sticky rice for dessert.

When they walked out of the restaurant, headed for their separate cars, the woman asked if he'd like to come over to her apartment for coffee. It took everything he had not to laugh in her face.

On the drive home, he asked himself why he bothered anymore. Even if he found someone who was a good match for him, he would never have been able to open up to her. His job was okay, but he was getting tired of teaching disengaged twenty-somethings who could barely be bothered to look up from their phone screens. And why the fuck had he decided to go into sociology in the first place? To study humanity? As if he were an outsider, an alien, who could never understand what it was like to be human, no matter how hard he tried?

For the first time in his life, a thought crosses his mind.

Maybe Dad had the right idea.

Fuck it. He already feels miserable. He might as well get up and go grade some essays . . .

After a little hair of the dog, that is.

THE MEMORIES END, AND ONCE MORE, HE FINDS himself facing his mother, father, and other self. Young

Lewis has returned to his chair and his immobility, and the crowd continues chanting, insisting on his worthlessness.

"All living things have an innate desire – a deep, desperate longing – for their own death," Dad says. *"It is, after all, what life is created for in the first place: to end. This death wish is embodied in the Unhigh."*

Lewis' younger self remains still and unblinking, but now it smiles.

"I introduced you to it when you were a child, and I brought you back several times so that the two of you could . . . become close."

"Normally, the Unhigh is patient," Mom says. *"Why shouldn't it be? All life comes to it in the end, whether willingly or not. But things are different now. Do you know how many people are on the planet today?"*

The sudden shift of topic confuses Lewis for a second, but then he answers.

"Close to eight billion, I think."

"And more are being born every instant," Dad says. *"At this point, speaking in terms of combined weight, there are more humans on the planet than there are animals."*

"It's not sustainable," Mom says. *"If something isn't done, soon the entire world will become unlivable."*

Lewis looks at his mother and father, sweeps his gaze around the meat-room to take in the Unhighs's congregation. Are any of them who they appear to be? Or all they all merely masks for the Unhigh, including his mom and dad?

You're a smart one, the shotgun says, *but I've always known that.*

Lewis' double grins, as if in agreement.

"What do you want from me?" he asks.

"If everything dies, then so does death itself," Dad says. *"The herd needs to be culled before it can do irreparable damage to the planet. But in order to act on a large scale in the physical world, the Unhigh must have an avatar."*

He gestures toward Young Lewis, who is still grinning.

"So much has been done to prepare you," Mom says. *"Some real, some less so. Your visits to the shrine, your father's suicide, the deaths of your classmates in high school . . . All were arranged to prepare your psyche to accept the Unhigh. Even so, you weren't ready until this morning, when you woke and for the first time truly considered humanity's age-old question – to be or not to be."*

"And this is why people in town started killing themselves?" Lewis says. "Because for a moment, I threw myself a pity party?"

"Yes," Dad says. *"It was enough to tip the scales in the Unhigh's favor, and it could begin its work. But its*

influence is confined to this town. In order for it to spread, it must join with you. The two of you must become one."

Lewis is getting tired of this game. He focuses his attention on his younger self – on the Unhigh – since that's who he's truly talking with.

"Then why not just take me and get it over with?"

It only works if you give yourself willingly, the shotgun says. *You must* desire *death for the Unhigh to claim you.*

"What if I press the muzzle of this shotgun beneath my chin and blow my brains out? You won't have anything to possess then."

"By killing yourself, you'll be surrendering to the Unhigh," Mom says, *"and it will have you."*

Lewis shoulders the shotgun and aims it at his younger self's forehead.

"And what if I blow out my other me's brains?"

"Then you would also be killing yourself," Dad says, *"and the Unhigh would still win."*

Lewis closes one eye to sharpen his aim, tightens his finger on the trigger . . . It would be so easy, just one shot, and the nightmare his life has become would be over. He remains that way for several long moments, holding his breath, unsure what he's going to do, but then a question occurs to him.

"If I'm so goddamned worthless, why do you want

me so badly?"

The crowd's chanting dies away. No one answers, not his father, not his mother, not the weapon in his hand. The silence continues for several moments, then he lowers the shotgun.

"Maybe there are too many people in the world, and maybe the planet would be better off if there were fewer of us. I don't know. What I *do* know is that life means possibility. Sure, things might get worse, but they might get better. Right now, my life sucks, but suicide is a permanent solution to what I hope is a temporary problem. And that's what you'd take away from people – hope. I won't help you do that."

Lewis relaxes his grip on the shotgun, releases it, and it falls to the meat-floor with a soft *plap*.

What are you doing? the gun shouts. *Pick me up! Use me! It's what you were born for!*

His mother and father are scowling, and his other self is no longer grinning.

"It's my life, and I'll decide what to do with it. Not you, not anyone else. Dark voices may speak to us sometimes, tell us we're not good enough, that we're unlovable and worthless, that the world would be better off if we weren't in it. But those voices lie, and we don't have to listen to them, no matter how loud they are. And I don't have to listen to you. You're nothing but dumb, mindless hunger, greedy to glut yourself on all you can get."

His other self doesn't speak, but angry frustration flashes in his eyes.

"Don't do this!" Dad shouts.

"Stay!" Mom pleads.

Pick me up and use me! the shotgun begs.

"Fuck you all."

Lewis turns his back on them all and walks through the congregants toward the doorway. He expects them to come at him, grab hold of him, tear him apart in fury for betraying their master. But they merely watch without expression as he passes.

It's full dark by the time he exits Club Elite. The night air is crisp, the stars clear and bright, but so far away. He pauses by the door, reaches into his pocket, removes the Club Elite matchbook he picked up at his mom's building. He's tempted to go back inside, use the matches to set the place aflame, then stand in the parking lot and watch the motherfucker burn to ashes. He smiles, glances back at the building.

"Nice try."

He drops the matches to the ground and starts walking toward his car.

Afterword

I've heard the voice of the Unhigh before, and if you have too, here are some resources that might help you ignore its lies. Please reach out. The world needs all the good people it can get, and you're one of them.

– Tim

THE AMERICAN FOUNDATION FOR SUICIDE PREVENTION

https://afsp.org/suicide-prevention-resources

CANADIAN ASSOCIATION FOR SUICIDE PREVENTION

https://suicideprevention.ca/

SUICIDE HOTLINES AND CRISIS LINES IN THE UNITED KINGDOM

https://www.therapyroute.com/article/suicide-hotlines-and-crisis-lines-in-the-united-kingdom

SUICIDE PREVENTION AUSTRALIA

https://www.suicidepreventionaust.org/

ACKNOWLEDGMENTS

Thanks to Dan Franklin for making this book a reality, and as always, special thanks to my indefatigable agent Cherry Weiner.

About the Author

Four-time Bram Stoker Award winner Tim Waggoner has published over sixty novels and eight collections of dark fiction. He's also a full-time professor of creative writing and composition at Sinclair College in Dayton, Ohio.